MOUNTAIN MAN'S CAPTIVE

MEN OF MAPLE MOUNTAIN BOOK TWO

SADIE KING

Trapped in the woods and tied up by a mountain man...

First, he captures me in a hunting net, then he binds my wrists and feet to a chair.

I can't decide if this rugged mountain recluse is an axe murderer or a kind human trying to save me from myself.

What I do know, is one look and my body is on fire. I yearn to break free from my bindings and run my fingers through his thick beard.

Am I supposed to enjoy being held captive this much?

Mountain Man's Captive features an OTT obsessed mountain man and the curvy innocent woman he claims as his own. It's high heat, oh so sweet, and always with a happily ever after.

ANNIE

Branches scrape my arms as I stomp through the forest. My sweater catches on a bush, and I tug free, feeling the fabric tear.

Great, ruining my favorite sweater is another crime to add to Mark Granger's list of wrongs. Although alongside bullying and sexual assault, it's one of the lesser ones.

Tears sting my eyes and I wipe at them furiously; I will not let that asshole make me cry.

I can't believe I was stupid enough to let Mark Granger drive me up here.

Come see the stars with me, he said.

I know a great spot to watch the meteor shower, he said.

Now I'm halfway up the side of a mountain in the middle of the night with no way to get home to Maple Springs.

I glance at the sky, hoping to see the stars. If I can find Polaris, I can figure out which way I need to be heading to get back to the road.

All I see above me is blackness. I'm not sure if it's the canopy of trees or the thick storm clouds that have been gathering all day.

Mark told me it would clear up, that the storm would pass, and he had the perfect spot for star gazing.

Stupid, naive me believed him. I was too flattered that a boy had asked me out, because boys never ask me out. Least of all good-looking boys like Mark Granger.

Just because we're in astronomy club together, I trusted him.

I shouldn't have.

Once we got to this apparent star-gazing spot, he had his hands all over me. I told him no, but he wouldn't listen to my protests. He said I should be grateful. That a big girl like me wasn't going to get laid any other way.

But he didn't count on one thing, a big girl like me has strength. I kneed him in the balls, scrambled out from under him and gave him a punch on the nose for good measure.

That's when he swore at me, pushed me out of the car and drove off.

He left me here, halfway up the mountain in the dark. What kind of asshole does that?

A bird calls in the darkness and there's a snuffing noise to my left. I give a yelp and head to the right. I don't want to be some wild animal's dinner.

I waited for Mark to come back, not believing that he'd really leave me here. My phone must have dropped when he pushed me out and I couldn't find it in the dark. After a while, I realized he wasn't coming back.

In the dark it was hard to see the gravel road and after a while I lost it. So here I am, lost in the wood, in the middle of the night halfway up a mountain.

A sob escapes my lips and I grit my teeth and swallow down my hurt. I will not cry over this.

Through the trees I catch a glimpse of a warm orange glow.

My heart leaps. It's the first sign of human's I've seen since I've been wandering these woods.

It might be a house, or a cabin. Or it might be some crazy ass axe murderer.

I pause, the sounds of the woods mingle with my heavy breathing and the blood pounding in my ears. A cool breeze rattles through the trees and I wrap my arms around myself to fight off the cold.

An animal howls in the distance.

That does it. Deciding I'd rather take my chances with an axe murderer then spend the night out here alone, I head toward the light.

As I get closer, I can make out a log cabin sitting on its own in a clearing. Who the hell lives out here alone in the woods?

Treading carefully, I sneak toward the clearing, scanning the property for clues as to who lives here, friend or foe.

Running the side of the cabin are raised vegetable beds and a line of fruit trees. The light from the window falls on the trees illuminating plump red apples.

I relax a little. An axe murderer wouldn't have an apple orchard. Would he?

Moving forward, I'm almost at the clearing when I stumble over what at first seems like a tree root.

There's a clicking noise, and then the sound of

rope rubbing along bark. Something closes around my foot and I let out a scream as I'm thrown upside down.

My head never hits the ground because as I fall, I'm pulled sideways and into the air. The rope closes around me and I'm swinging, upside down, trapped in a thick rope net.

Oh god, I'm caught by an axe murderer.

A scream pierces the night and penetrates the walls of my cabin.

Grabbing my gun from its rack, I pause to check the security cameras. The infrared picks up something hovering off the ground on the edge of my perimeter.

One of the traps has been sprung and there's something inside, dangling from a tree.

I'm not sure what I've caught that makes that kind of high-pitched scream. It looks too big for a raccoon. Could be a bear, but they seldom come down this far.

I catch a flash of a leg and an arm protruding through the rope.

"Shit."

Hitting zoom on the camera I go closer to see what I've caught.

"I'll be damned."

Wriggling in the net like a caught fish, is a woman.

Her hair is splayed out around wide eyes and the plumpest bee stung lips. Her body is pressed against the rope and I get a flash of heavy breasts and a curvy ass.

"Holy shit."

She's gorgeous. The breath goes out of me and a strange sensation runs through my body making me hot all over.

I'm transfixed by her image on my screen. What is this beauty doing on my mountain in the dark and how the hell did she wander onto my property?

Grabbing my head torch and strapping it round my forehead, I venture out to see what I've caught.

My light pierces the darkness of the forest illuminating my path to the trap. The beam sweeps over the net picking up her upside-down body, caught awkwardly in the trap.

"My boyfriend's hiding in the woods with a shotgun trained on you."

Her words make me pause. Boyfriend. I don't

like the sound of that. Even though she's lying through her teeth.

"I'm not gonna hurt you."

She snorts. "I'm upside down and caught in your trap. Already hurting."

"If you stop wriggling, I'll let you down."

"You take one more step toward me and he'll shoot."

I move toward her and crouch so I'm eye level. She's got the deepest brown eyes and they're blazing with anger. There's no gunshot.

"Let me down, you monster."

She flails her arms and one of them slips through the rope, causing her to roll forwards.

The more she thrashes, the tighter the rope pulls around her, until she's bundled up like a cute bale of hay.

But I can't release the rope until she's still, otherwise she'll go crashing to the ground.

I sit back on my haunches and wait for her to stop wriggling.

Finally, she gives up. Her arm trails almost on the ground and she looks at me with a wary eye.

"If you're going to kill me, just get it over with."

She looks resigned to her fate, which almost makes me laugh.

"I'm not gonna kill you."

She eyes me warily. "That's exactly what an axe murderer would say."

"Do I look like an axe murderer?"

Her eyes travel over me and I feel heat under her gaze.

"Yes. You're a big, bearded man with a gun slung over his shoulder who lives alone, I assume, on the side of a mountain. It's the MO of an axe murderer."

I chuckle, and the sound surprises myself. I spend so much of my time alone I barely get an opportunity to laugh.

"I'm glad you think it's funny. Or are you stupid too?"

Wow, this woman's got a mouth on her. She's bold for someone who's swinging upside down from a tree.

"Now that wasn't nice."

I stand up getting ready to cut her down when the beam from my light sweeps over her body.

Her leggings are torn giving me a glimpse of a silky pale calf. In the beam of the torch, I trace the line of her body. Plump ass, curvy as hell. Even all pushed up and awkward looking in my net I can tell she's beautiful.

My cock stirs, a sensation I've not felt in a long time. Of all the times to get a hard on. That'll scare her even more. At least she won't be able to see in the dark.

I pull my hunting knife out of its sheath on my belt and she screams.

Goddamn, what does she think I'm going to do, hurt her or something? I already know I'd never hurt this beauty.

With a quick movement, I slice through the rope that's holding the net up. It crashes down, unfurling the net and disgorging its precious catch. I'm standing underneath, and she falls right into my arms. She's so surprised it knocks the scream right out of her.

Her huge brown eyes look startled. There are scratches on her face and her clothes are torn. That didn't happen from hanging out in my rope trap.

"Where did you come from little fish?"

Her mouth flops open and closed but she doesn't speak. Her body presses against me and it feels so good, so natural, like she belongs there.

"Let's go inside and get you cleaned up."

Reluctantly I lower her to the ground so I can

retrieve my knife. I'm slinging it into my belt when there's a shooting pain in my shin.

She kicked me. I spin around in time to see her disappearing through the trees. God knows where she thinks she's going but there's a sharp cliff face another hundred feet or so that way and there's a storm about to hit. I can't let her run around my mountain in the dark, it's too dangerous.

Catching up easily I put a hand on her shoulder. "Hey."

The kick comes out of nowhere and she's got me in the shin again.

The girls got some spirit in her. But she's heading to danger and I can't have her running blindly through the forest.

"I'm not going to hurt you."

"Let me go."

She tries to shake my hand off her but I'm too strong.

"Can't do that. Too dangerous."

She's struggling to be free and though I hate what I'm about to do, it's the only way stop her running into danger.

"You're gonna hate me for this."

In one quick movement I catch around the

waist. She gives a surprised yelp as I sling her over my shoulder.

"Put me down."

Her fists pummel my back.

"Nope."

My arm wraps around her legs, pinning them against me so she can't kick. Her mound is pressed against my shoulder and I catch a musky scent, the scent of her.

My nostrils quiver and it's like an electric shot straight to my dick. It stands to attention and now I do feel like the bad man of the mountain, but Christ, this woman's got my body going all sorts of crazy.

"I'm not going to hurt you, sweetheart. But the mountain side is no place to be in the dark."

There's been a storm brewing all day and as I stride to the cabin, the first thick raindrops hit my face.

I push open the door to my cabin and she stops wiggling. I'm hoping she sees that it's a safe place.

There's a fire burning in the grate and the smell of roast chicken from the dinner I just ate permeates the cabin.

I carry her to the fire.

"If I let you down, do you promise not to run?"

"Fine."

As she slides off my shoulder her breasts press against my body and a wave of desire washes over me. Christ, if she knew what I was thinking…

"Sorry about…" My words are cut short as she makes a break for the door. I move quicker then she does and block the entrance.

"It's not safe out there."

I try to explain but she's got a determined look about her and she's eyeing up my shins. I'm pretty sure her kicks could be lethal to a smaller man. But I'm not a small man, I'm six foot six and as thick as the mountain I live on.

"Let me out of here." Her eyes flash anger and I really hate doing this but there's no way I'm letting her wander about out there in the dark. Even if she hates me for it.

"Nope. Not in the dark."

Capturing her up in my arms there's only one thing to do.

Slinging her over my shoulder again I carry her to my supply cupboard.

"Let me go, you brute."

Her fists pummel my back

"I don't like to do this to you. But it's for your own safety."

There's a shelf full of rope and I grab a thin one, perfect for binding. With my leg, I swing one of the wooden chairs toward the fire and plonk her on it.

Her head twists wildly and when she sees the rope her eyes widen.

"You're not seriously going to tie me up?"

She sounds incredulous.

"Yup. Until you learn to listen to me and let me keep you safe."

I stand astride her, keeping her legs pinned together while I bind her arms. I must concentrate on what I'm doing and not the curvy woman below me or I'll get hard and then she really will have something to scream about.

She's peering at me now and I feel the scrutiny of her gaze.

"Is this how you treat all the women who visit your cabin?"

"Only the ones who are hellbent on killing themselves in a storm."

With her hands bound behind her, I bend down and work on her legs, binding the ankles together.

Satisfied she won't be able to break free I stand up. The fire's warm on the back of my legs. But that's not the only thing making me hot. with her hands behind her, her tits are pushed put showing off two voluptuous mounds.

Too bad she's looking at me like she wants to kill me. I'm really trying not to be the bad guy here, but I know this doesn't look good.

"I hate doing this, but if you go out in that storm tonight, you won't survive."

I'm not sure if she hears me. She's breathing hard and her anger is palpable. I don't blame her.

I've just met the woman of my dreams and I've got her tied up in my cabin. I'm pretty sure this is the shittiest seduction ever.

3

ANNIE

Rope rubs at my wrists as I wriggle my hands trying to get free.

Of all the shitty luck. the one cabin I stumble across is a freakin axe murderer. Except he's wearing a knitted sweater with a moose on it and he's got a kindly smile. Not how I imagined a murderer would look.

The man is speaking but I can't hear what he's saying over the sound of the blood thumping in my ears.

Something about a storm.

He watches me with a frown on his face. His cool blue eyes peek out of his rugged beard. When he had me over this shoulder, I could feel his beard scratching against my thighs where my leggings had ripped.

It caused a ripple through my tummy and a damp sensation between my legs that was so confusing it made me thrash even more.

Now he's watching me intently and I feel it again. A tug, deep in my core. My body shivers and something weird happens to my nipples. They're hardening and I hope to God, he can't see them through my shirt.

Are you supposed to get turned on by the man holding you captive? But he was so gentle when he tied me up and apologetic. Is that some weird murderer thing they do?

He's got his arms folded and seems to be waiting for me to do something. I'm not sure what. He looks exasperated. Maybe I'm not behaving like most of his victims.

But then I've never been in a situation where I'm about to get murdered so I'm not sure how to behave.

The rope isn't done up too tight, but I can tell there's no way I'm getting it loose. Suddenly feeling exhausted, I stop struggling.

"There's a storm coming. You can't go out there."

He's speaking slowly, like I'm a child. But finally, I get what he's saying.

There's a storm. I shouldn't go out in it; I need to stay here in his remote cabin alone with him. He'll keep me safe. Sounds plausible, but it also sounds exactly like what an axe murderer would say.

As if to back him up, a smattering of rain hits the window. I glance over to it and back at him.

"See, a storm." He points.

My body slackens. Maybe he is telling the truth? Maybe I'm safer here with him then out there in the rain.

"I'm not going to hurt you. You got caught in my net."

Or maybe not. He did set a trap to catch me.

"What's the net for?"

He pulls one of the other chairs around and sits opposite me.

"Racoons mostly. They kill my chickens. Sometimes I catch a wood hen. I've never caught a woman before."

There's a smile playing on his lips and his eyes are dancing in a way that makes me want to touch him. If only my hands were free.

"My name's Colton. You're in my cabin. You'll be safe in here."

I snort. "Safe? I'm tied up."

"Yeah." He rubs his beard. "I know that looks bad. But I'm keeping you safe."

The rope presses against my skin and with the way he's looking at me and my breasts pressed forward like this, it is causing a strange sensation to creep over my skin. A hot itch, a longing. Surely not for this brute?

His gaze travels over my legs and I feel a tug of desire. I press my thighs together, trying to banish it.

"You're bleeding. I'll get the first aid kit."

While he's out of the room I scan my surroundings. On the ledge above the fire are pictures. Him with an arm around an older woman who I guess is his mother.

Another one with a bunch of guys in a fishing boat. Holding up decent size fish. I squint at the pictures. One of the guys looks familiar, I've seen him working in the bar down the mountain.

Relief floods over me. Colton may just be a regular guy who likes solitude. Then I notice the gun rack above the door. And next to it a set of three knives.

There's no axe, but at least one of the knives looks big enough to chop up a body.

Oh shit. I've got to get out of here.

Colton comes back into the room and I quickly look away from the wall of death.

He crouches next to me and sets the first aid kit and a tub of water on the floor.

"This might sting."

My pulse is racing and I'm not sure if it's because I'm scared or turned on. Is he or isn't he going to kill me?

Gently, he presses the cloth against my bleeding leg. His touch is so tender and the look on concern on his face so genuine.

"You live here alone?"

"Yup, just me and the chickens."

Oh great, so no one will hear me scream.

"I'm completely self-sufficient."

For a moment I forget he's maybe an axe murderer. I have a vision of him tending the orchard I saw and clearing land with his bare hands.

"That sounds nice."

He smiles and I look away. Damn, I'm not here to have a conversation, the man's tied me up for Christ's sake, I'm angry at him. Only he is exceptionally hot, kind, and tending gently to my wounds.

"You got a name?"

I'm not willing to tell him that yet so I remain silent. After a few moments he tries again.

"What were you doing out in the woods on your own?"

The last thing I want to do is tell this man about my stupidity. How naive I was to be lured out here so a teenage boy from astronomy club could try to take advantage of me.

I close my lips.

"You don't want to tell me that's fine."

He finishes dabbing at the blood and rubs a salve into the wounds.

"How do your wrists feel?"

I narrow my eyes at him.

"My wrists hurt."

It's only partly true. They ache a little and there's something nice about being tied up with this man looking at me that I'm enjoying. But the knives have me creeped out and this could be my chance to get away.

"If I untie these. Are you going to promise not to run off into the dark?"

Keeping my face straight, I nod.

"Because there's a cliff face not too far from here and record rainfall expected tonight. I need to keep you safe."

"I promise."

I cross my fingers behind my back. Because even though this man has a gentle touch and is doing things to my body I don't understand, there's no way I'm sticking around to find out if he's a murderer or not. He must be near an access road and if I can find that I can find the main road and get home.

He unsheathes the huge knife that he keeps round his belt and slashes through the bindings on my legs. As they fall away, he comes round the back and frees my hands.

I stand up slowly, stretching the tension out of my wrists.

"I'll go dump this water."

He goes through the door to what I guess is the bathroom. As soon as he's through the door, I make a break for it.

Sprinting across the room, I pull open the front door. Rain lashes my face and a bolt of thunder booms overhead making me jump.

I hesitate, this storm looks mean, I could get

lost in it, never find my way out. Maybe Colton is just a good guy trying to keep me safe.

A flash of lighting follows the thunder illuminating my surroundings and I glimpse the access road that would lead me home.

If I'm going to go, I need to go now. Wondering if I'm being incredibly stupid, I bolt down the steps and into the night.

4

COLTON

The sound of the door banging brings me back to the living room. It's wide open, the rain falling in sheets against the dark sky. The woman is nowhere to be seen.

"Damn."

She won't last ten minutes in this weather. Striding to the door I fix my head lamp back on my forehead.

"Hey!"

The rain drowns out my voice. Not that she'll come to me anyway. Am I really that frightening that she'd prefer to be out here alone then safe in the cabin with me?

My feet carry me down the steps and I cross the yard, moving my head from left to right to illuminate the area. The driving rain makes it hard to see anything.

A tightness constricts my chest thinking about her out here alone.

My feet trip over something and I stumble. In the beam of my torch, I find her, crouched on the ground and shivering with mud streaks down her face. She must have fallen.

She looks up at me with doleful eyes, the look tugging at my heart.

My arms go around her and this time she doesn't resist as I lift her up.

"You're okay, sweetheart."

Her hair hangs in wet clumps around her mud-streaked face and she burrows it into my shoulder.

I carry her inside and sit her on the chair, this time not using restraints. Her wet clothes cling to her body showing off every curve. I have to look away before I lose it.

Water drips off her forming puddles on the floor and she hangs her head.

"If you're going to murder me, can you just get it over and done with."

Christ, does she still really think I'm dangerous?

"I'm not going to murder you."

I hold out my phone.

"Go ahead and call whoever you need to call. The road into town is closed so you'll have to stay here with me for the night.

My name's Colton Bray. And I live at Wildwood Cabin. Tell them to call the ranger, Kit, if they want to check I'm legit."

She looks at the phone suspiciously. "You have signal up here?"

"Living off the grid doesn't mean shunning technology. I've got my own satellite dish."

She looks at me wearily like there's something else she wants to say.

"Why are you wearing a moose sweater?"

A smile plays on my lips. "My mother knitted it for me. I wasn't expecting company."

The answer seems to satisfy her and she relaxes and takes the phone.

While she makes a call, I head to the bedroom to change into dry clothes. I can hear her talking to someone and when I come back to the room, she's looking sheepish.

"They've closed the road into town for fear of washouts."

Just like I told her.

"Do you believe me now? That you're better off

in my cabin than wondering round out there on your own?"

She looks away and bites her bottom lip. It's fucking adorable and I feel a rush of protectiveness over her. She's walked onto my property and that makes me responsible for her.

"I spoke to my mom," she says, "apparently she knows you."

I wonder who her mom is. There's not a lot of people I have much to do with these days.

"Or she knows of you. She's seen you at Bear's."

Bear's Brewery, it's the bar in the little mountain town halfway between here and Maple Springs. My buddy Bear owns it and I go there occasionally for a drink.

"You live with your mom?"

She nods.

Christ, I'm lusting over this woman and I don't even know if she's legal.

"How old are you?"

"I'm eighteen."

Holy shit, I've got twelve years on her. The protective feeling grows stronger.

She's mine to look after, mine to protect.

"Your mom doesn't need to worry; I'll deliver you home safe as soon as this storm clears."

She looks up at me, her eyes wide and for the first time there's no fear in them. I guess she finally trusts me.

"Thank you."

She's dripping muddy water on the floor and starting to shiver.

"You need to get cleaned up and warm."

I hand her a towel and point her in the direction of the bathroom. "Shower's through that door."

She's pulls open the bathroom door and then stops and turns around.

"Annie, my name's Annie."

I try out the sound on my lips, but already the door's shutting behind her.

"Annie."

She'll be peeling off her wet clothes, pulling her shirt over heavy tits.

I dig my nails into my palms and try not to think about the naked goddess in my bathroom.

To distract myself I head to the kitchen. She must be hungry and I get to work cooking an omelet.

She's still not told me what the hell she was doing on her own crashing through the forest at night. If someone's hurt her, they'll have me to answer to.

The shower turns off and a few minutes later the bathroom door opens. She's wearing one of my shirts, which is like an oversize dress on her, trailing all the way to her knees. As she towels her wet hair the hem creeps up giving me a view of her thick thighs.

I turn away quickly adjusting my dick. Does she have any idea what effect she's having on me?

With a monumental effort, I still my racing blood. She's only just starting to trust me; I can't scare her now with a giant hard on.

When I've got my dick under control, I set the omelets on the table in front of her.

"Did you make this for me?"

Her delight is palpable. She gives me a smile and peeps up at me through lowered lashes turning my heart to liquid and my cock to steel.

She's mine.

The thought comes into my head and it's too right and so natural.

As I watch her eat, my fist clenches impatiently.

This little fish got caught in my net for a reason. I may not be an axe murderer, but that doesn't mean I won't ravage her.

5

ANNIE

Colton's staring at me intently over the table. It's a look that makes me feel giddy and flushed all over. I don't understand what this feeling is but I like it.

"So, um what do you do out here?"

I chatter nervously trying to calm the heat between my legs.

"Raise chickens, hunt, live off the land."

It seems idyllic and I let out an involuntary sigh.

"Sounds amazing. Is it lonely?"

He leans on the table so his beard trails the tabletop. How I long to run my fingers through the bristly hair. I wonder if it will be coarse or soft.

"No."

It's a definite answer and I cock my head, waiting for him to give me more.

"People can be assholes; I don't miss them."

I'm reminded of Mark, who left me out here all alone.

"You can say that again."

His eyes narrow. "Did someone hurt you, little fish?"

The nickname makes me smile; no one's ever called me little before. Then I notice his clenched fists and I understand in an instant, if I told him about Mark, he'd hunt him down and hurt him. Hurt him bad, maybe even kill him.

My head swims, I feel a rush of warmth, that this big strong man would do that for me. But also, um, reality. However much of an asshole Mark is, I don't want his death on my conscious.

"This omelet is good."

He sits back and I sense his frustration at me changing the subject, but he doesn't push.

"The eggs were laid this morning."

"Really? These are your eggs?" I savor the next mouthful, taking in the rich taste.

"You can meet the girls tomorrow, help me feed them. There's usually a couple of eggs every morning."

Spending my days with chickens instead of people sounds idyllic. I have a vision of life up here. Tending to the orchard, feeding the chickens, and at night watching the stars. Not having to bother with anyone else but ourselves.

Colton takes my plate to the kitchen and I watch him go. A few hours ago, I was terrified of the man, now I'm contemplating a life with him. What the hell is wrong with me?

My body feels weary and maybe my mind is going too, that must be it, exhaustion.

Involuntarily I let out a big unattractive yawn.

"You need some sleep."

He's not wrong. It's been an eventful few hours and after a hot shower and some food, I'm ready to crash.

As if reading my mind, Colton comes round to my side of the table. He leans forward.

"What are you doing?"

Before I know what's happening, he's scooped me up in his arms.

"Relax, I'm taking you to bed.'

My body melts against him and I press my face into his shirt. It's rough, woolen fabric and smells like wood and fresh rain.

My eyes close as I let him carry me into the

bedroom. He pulls the duvet down and deposits me between the sheets.

For a wild moment I think he's going to climb in next to me. There's that tug again, a yearning in my core that I can't explain.

Then he pulls the covers up to my chin and kisses my forehead. A chaste gentle kiss before he backs away.

"Goodnight little fish."

The last thing I see is his figure outlined in the darkness as he switches the light off, then sleep claims me.

6

COLTON

I t's early the next morning when Annie shuffles into the living room rubbing sleep out of her eyes. Her hair falls around her shoulders in messy waves and she looks so fresh, so innocent that I think my heart might explode.

I don't know what brought her onto my property, but with every moment we spend together, I don't want her to leave.

"Morning gorgeous." She gives me a confused look as I hand her a coffee mug.

"No one's ever called me that before."

I'm stunned. She is the most beautiful creature I've ever seen, how anyone could not see that is beyond me.

"Then they're blind."

She furrows her brows at me. "Or you are."

It annoys me, this putting down of herself. I can sense it comes from years of teasing, probably about her weight. She doesn't realize how beautiful she is, and her curvy figure is part of that. There's work to do, filling my little fish with confidence. It won't happen immediately, but I'll make her feel good about herself every opportunity I can.

"You wanna help feed the chickens?"

She slips into a pair of my old gumboots, which are so big they look like clown shoes on her, but after the rain last night, the ground is muddy.

I take her on a tour of my property, showing her the raised beds where I grow enough vegetables all year round to never have to visit the shops. She meets Tracey, the goat, who provides fresh milk, and my five fat hens.

She asks intelligent questions and I get the sense she's not just being polite; she's genuinely interested in what I've got going on up here. That fills me with hope.

I want her so much to like it. More than like it, I want her to love it. I want her to be a part of what I'm doing here.

I show her the solar panels that Tony helped me install last year. They provide enough energy so I can live off grid with my own electricity supply.

Her face glows with each new thing and I have a vision of her here with me. Tending the garden, her pregnant belly protruding.

The sound of a car engine pulls me out of my thoughts. I don't get many visitors, but it might be Brandon, needing help with clearing the roads after the storm.

A car comes into view. A white sports car, with a kid behind the wheel. It looks out of place on the mountain.

"Wait in the house sweetheart." I turn to Annie and she's frozen. A look of fear on her face.

"You know this guy?"

She opens her mouth and closes it again. When she speaks it's a whisper. "Mark."

My gut clenches. I don't like the sound of this. "He your boyfriend or something?" It comes out as a growl.

She shakes her head. "No."

The kid gets out of the car and I go to meet him but she grabs hold of my shirt. "Don't let him see me." She darts behind the cabin and I stride forward.

He's a gangly kid, with sharp eyebrows and a mean stare, can't be more than nineteen years old. But if he's done something to hurt Annie, I'll kill him.

"Can I help you?"

He takes a step back as I walk toward him. My fists clench at my sides and I make no effort to hide my distrust.

"Have you seen a girl?"

I'm sure he's talking about Annie, but I'm not handing her over to this mug.

"Why, you lost one?"

She snorts as if it's a funny joke. "Yeah, last night."

I fix him with a steely look and he squirms under my gaze.

"How do you lose a girl?"

He rubs his nose and glances away. "She jumped out of the car."

This guy's lying through his teeth.

"Now, what you doing to a girl to make her jump out of your car?"

He looks around nervously, and he should be nervous. I'll break his fucking neck.

"Um, I broke down. She ran off. But I can't find her."

So, this fuck knuckle is the guy responsible for leaving Annie out on her own all night.

"You left Annie out here, on her own?"

Relief washes over his face.

"So, you have seen her, phew. I got home and then felt bad, like she might get eaten by a bear or something, so I tried to come back to…"

He doesn't get a chance to finish. My fingers grab his throat and I push him back against the hood of his car.

"You left a woman out here on her own at night."

His eyes bulge.

"I came back for her."

His voice shakes with fear, which is good. I want him to quake, I want him to be so scared he shits himself.

"In the middle of a fucking storm. She could have died out here you useless piece of shit."

His mouth falls open and closed again.

Anything could have happened to Annie out there if I hadn't have found her. A red haze fills my vision, my hand closes around his throat.

"I'll fucking kill you." It will feel good to

squeeze his neck till it snaps for leaving my girl like that.

"Colton, stop."

Annie's voice cuts through my anger.

"Colton, he's not worth it."

She's at my side laying her small hand on my arm. "Don't kill him please." Her calm touch makes me pause. I look at her pleading face. She's right, this asshole isn't worth the jail time.

I loosen my grip.

"You're lucky she's a better person then you'll ever be." I release the guy's neck and he doubles over, gasping for air.

"I won't kill you, out of respect for Annie's wishes. But I will beat the shit out of you."

I pull him up by his collar and my fist connects with his face. There's the satisfying sound of bone breaking which will ruin his pretty boy nose.

"That's for leaving Annie up here." He stumbles back clutching his nose. "And if you ever touch her again, I really will kill you."

He stumbles backwards to the car and fumbles with the door.

"Now get the fuck off my mountain."

The ignition starts and the wheels skid as he

takes off reversing all the way down my access road.

Satisfied he's gone I turn to Annie. She's trembling and I fold her in my arms.

"I will kill him if you ask me to Annie."

She shakes her head. "You don't need to do that."

She's looking at the ground and taking her cheeks in my hands I pull her face up so she's looking at me.

"I would kill for you Annie, anything you ask. You're mine, you understand. And I protect what's mine."

Her breathing becomes shallow and her eyes wide. I've just laid out my feelings for her and my body tenses as I wait for her to respond. It feels like an age before her lips part and she says the sweetest words I could ever hear.

"You're mine too."

My lips crash into hers and it's like a storm crashing around us. The air crackles with energy and I put my whole being into the kiss. Showing her with my touch what she means to me.

Her body presses against me, causing an instant rise of blood through my veins and straight to my cock.

My hardness grinds against her and she pushes back, her hips moving against me.

I put a hand either side of her hips and lift her up. She wraps her legs around me, and still joined at the mouth, I carry her into my cabin.

7

ANNIE

My body pulses with energy and heat as Colton carries me inside. He would have killed Mark if I'd given the word, I have no doubt about that. And that thrills me. That this big strong man would do anything for me.

I squeeze my feet together and push my hips into him, making him groan.

"Annie, you're driving me wild."

He lays me down on the bed and stares down at me, his eyes hooded and intense. I feel confident under his gaze, confident enough to slide the shirt of his I'm wearing up my thighs so he can see the secret I've been carrying all night and all morning.

My underwear was soaked after the rain last

night, when I got dressed in his shirt, I didn't put any panties on.

He gasps as I lift the cotton, revealing my sex to him. My fingers run through the hair and come away slick.

"Oh sweetheart."

His dick is already pushing through his trousers and now he slides them off, revealing a thick cock, which glistens with pre-cum.

My breathing goes up a notch and I think I'm going to pass out. I'm way out my depth here with a dick that big.

He must see my wide-eyed stare because he chuckles.

"Don't worry little fish, you'll get used to it."

He slides his knee between my legs and climbs onto the bed.

I prop myself up on my elbows because this is probably the time to tell him I'm new to all this.

"Um." I begin, but his mouth closes around my ear and it sends shivers all the way down to my pussy.

My words turn to moans.

"What's that sweetheart?"

He kisses my neck and I tilt my head to the side, wanting more.

"I, um."

His hand grabs the shirt front and he pulls it open. buttons pings across the room and the heat of his breath glides over my breasts.

"Oh god that's good."

His beard tickles my nipples and I know it's soft. Soft with a spring to it that brushes over my nipples making them hard.

I moan again.

His hand slides down my belly and over my mound and then his fingers are tangled in my hair, spreading my lips apart and brushing my entrance.

"You're so wet."

His finger slides along my entrance and then inside. My body bucks at the sensation and he groans.

"You're so tight."

"Because I'm a virgin." I finally mange to blurt out.

He freezes and I'm worried I've done something wrong. His fingers stop moving and a whimper escapes my lips.

"Is that okay?" I whisper.

"Oh sweetheart. That's more than okay. That's fucking amazing."

There's something else I want to say, though

I'm not sure how to. As if reading my mind, he raises his eyebrows.

"What is it honey?"

I bite my lip, not sure how to ask for what I need. "You know when you tied me up last night?"

He nods slowly. "Yeah. And I apologize. It was the only way to stop you taking off into the storm."

I shake my head impatiently. "I know, it's fine."

He cocks his head. "Then what is it?"

"I um, I kinda liked it."

Realization dawns on his face and his eyes light up.

"You want me to tie you up?"

I feel silly asking, but the thought of Colton having his way with me while I'm restrained causes a gush of wetness between my legs.

I nod my head.

He chuckles. "Let me get the rope."

A few minutes later I'm completely naked with a hand tied to either side of the bed post. I've never felt so exposed, but also so safe.

Colton strips naked and stands in front of me, his gaze sweeping over my entire body.

"You are gorgeous Annie."

It doesn't feel as stupid as the first time he said

it, and I think maybe, just maybe, he might believe it's true.

The thought makes me bold and I move my legs, slowly opening them up and exposing myself to him.

He watches, mesmerized as I let my thighs fall open.

His breathing goes shallow as he kneels before me. "I'm going to make sure you never forget your first time."

His promise is followed by a slow kiss as his hand sweeps up my body. His mouth moves slowly, travelling down my neck, toying with my nipples. I pull at my restraints longing to run my fingers through his hair, but they hold fast.

It's exquisite torture as his kisses travel further south, over my belly and to my sex. When his mouth connects with my pussy, I cry out. It's like volts of electricity are running through my veins, turning my blood hot.

Then his tongue licks my hard nub and I almost come undone. My nerve endings zing to life making my legs spasm.

I pull at my bindings, wanting to run my hands through his hair, to move his head back and forth over me. But I can't move, I must go at his pace and he's going so exquisitely slow.

A finger glides into my opening and then another.

The pressure is building, so slowly, but I want it all now.

"Go faster."

He pauses and looks up at me and that's worse.

"Go faster."

There's a begging note to my voice. He sits back on his haunches and fixes me with a lazy smile.

My pussy aches for attention and I want to pull him back down. I pull at my hands but they stay fast.

"You didn't say the magic word."

He's teasing me and by the hardness of his cock, enjoying my frustration. I'll say anything he wants right now as long as he puts his mouth back over my pussy.

"Please, Colton. Please, go faster."

I writhe my hips, bucking toward him, longing to feel his mouth on me again.

He captures my hips and holds them in the air.

"Anything for you little fish."

His tongue laps at my clit and while one hand

holds my hips in the air, the other slides into me, one, two, three fingers.

I'm on the edge of pleasure and I teeter there for a moment before I fall over the top. Stars burst in my vision and I scream out his name as pleasure rips through me. I never knew I could feel like this, feel so good.

But he's not done. His mouth presses against me and I come again, bucking and writhing until I think I can't stand it anymore.

As the second orgasm wains, he climbs on top of me.

"You're ready."

He kisses my mouth and I taste my own saltiness. The rope bites at my wrist as I tug on them, wanting to touch him, but loving the restraint of not being able to.

He throws my leg over his shoulder and pulls my hips upwards, meeting his cock.

I'm at his complete mercy and can only watch as he positions me like a rag doll. His cock lining up with my entrance. The tip running over my glistening lips.

I moan, a guttural sound that I don't recognize as my own voice.

"This might hurt a little."

I don't have time to respond before he pushes inside me. There's a searing pain and then an intense throbbing as my pussy adjusts to his size.

He bends my legs towards my chest and sinks into me further. His hand runs over my nipples and I push my tits out to meet his touch.

"You okay sweetheart?"

I'm so lost in a world of new sensations that I can barely speak.

"Yah-hah."

"Good cause I'm going to fuck you hard."

The words send a shiver through me. My hips buck and I meet his every thrust. I wrap my legs around him, my heels digging into his back.

"Colton, I'm going to come again."

"Good. Come like a good girl."

Then I'm over the edge, and sliding into my orgasm, even more intense then the last.

I cry out his name and he tenses, groaning into my hair.

"Annie."

His hot liquid explodes into me, coating my walls and filling me up. We tremble together, sharing this pure moment as one.

Afterwards he unties me and holds me close.

"I never want you to leave." He murmurs,

tucking a strand of hair behind my ear. "Come live here, with me."

It seems like the most natural thing in the world and I snuggle into him. "Okay."

He holds me close and I know, I'll always be safe with my mountain man.

EPILOGUE

ANNIE

Six years later…

"You sure that's not going to hurt the baby?"

Colton's concern fights with his desire as he squares my hips over the chair.

My belly is even rounder than usual in the third trimester of pregnancy, and I'm horny as fuck. Which is why I sent the girls to their grandma's for the day.

"It won't hurt the baby if you go gentle with me."

His gaze flicks over the cleavage of my swollen breasts.

"I can't promise that sweetheart."

"Which is why I'm not taking any chances."

I swing my legs off him and pick up the rope that I left hidden under the table. Grabbing his hands, I pull them behind the chair.

"Hey, what're you doing?"

His shoulders pop forward and I loosen up a bit.

"Making sure you don't accidentally hurt the baby."

Pulling the rope tight I check my knot. It holds.

I walk slowly to the front of him and make a show of taking my top off. His dick tents in his pants. I unzip him and pull them off him.

"The day you got caught in my net, little fish, was the best day of my life."

I agree. It's six years since I moved in with Colton. Moved into our own little piece of paradise, far away from anyone else.

Molly arrived a year after and Angie eighteen months after that. Now there's a baby boy growing in my belly and I can't wait to meet him.

But my babies are the last thing on my mind as I hover over my husband's thick cock.

I lower myself gently, so only the tip slides inside me. Then I pause.

He growls and tugs at his restraints, impatient

to be inside me.

"Jesus, Annie, fuck me already."

I slide in another inch and he moans in frustration.

He tugs at the rope and the chair jerks nearly toppling us to the floor. A rope end flicks into the air and then his hands are on me. Pulling at my hips and sliding me down his shaft.

So much for the restraints.

His look is brutish and determined as he lifts me up and down his cock.

I push my hips to him, rubbing against him and feeling the pressure build.

"Fuck, Colton, I'm gonna come."

I explode and a moment later he does too. Impaling me on his cock and holding me in place as his seed shoots into me.

"That's not how that was supposed to go."

He grins.

"No? Then I suggest you get thicker rope."

He kisses my lips and wraps his arms around me and I lean into his chest.

After so long together, he's still my rock, my safe place and I know he always will be.

Complete the Men of Maple Mountain series for your swoon worthy OTT alphas.

Each book is a standalone but best enjoyed in together.

Men of Maple Mountain

Mountain Man's Obsession – Colette & Bear

Mountain Man's Captive – Annie & Colton

Mountain Man's Virgin – Brooklyn & Chase

Mountain Man's Muse – Heather & Kane

Mountain Man's Redemption – Bethany & Ewan

Mountain Man's First Time – Ursula & Kit

Companion titles

Mountain Man's Healer - Jenny & Rowan

All the Scars we Cannot See - Emily & Sam

Boxset Collection

Men of Maple Mountain Books 1-7

Includes a bonus short story:

Mountain Man's Steamy Anniversary - (Bear & Colette)

THE BIKER'S REVENGE

She's my enemy's daughter and my new obsession...

After three years inside, there's only one thing I want: revenge.

But when a retaliation goes wrong, I find myself with a fire cat captive—Scarlett, my enemy's daughter.

She's half my age and dripping with innocence. Scarlett becomes my revenge, and it's never been sweeter. But when her father comes for her, there's no way I'm giving her up.

The Biker's Revenge is a forbidden love, age-gap romance that starts with a kidnapping and ends with a happily ever after. Featuring an OTT obsessed hero and the curvy girl he claims as his own.

Keep reading for an exclusive excerpt or visit:
mybook.to/UCBikersRevenge

THE BIKER'S REVENGE

CHAPTER ONE

Bruno

The sound of smashing glass breaks the silence. Pans shakes out the rag that he wrapped around his wrist to break the window, sending shards of glass tumbling to the ground.

My eyes dart around the shadowy building, my ears straining for any sign that someone is inside.

But all is quiet at the Chaos Riders HQ. Our intel was correct. The club is on a run out of town, leaving their headquarters unprotected.

I don't expect to find much here, but we'll rough the place up, do as much damage as possible. I want Manny, the Chaos Riders' president, to know that I'm out, and I'm out for revenge.

I give a signal to the boys, and dark shapes emerge from the shadows. Pans is the first one in the window, and he clears the glass with a covered fist so no one gets cut as we climb through.

Flashing lights from the neon sign out front illuminate a bar with dancing poles leading up to the ceiling.

Lyle whistles. "Could get one of those installed at our place, Pres."

I shoot him a dark look. "You keep that in the strip club."

Lyle grins, but he knows I'm serious. My club is a place that's safe for women. There's a time and a place for a strip pole, and it's not front and center of our MC club.

"Where should we start?"

Jesse whistles softly as he twirls a baseball bat in his hand.

It's been a long time since I've been inside the Chaos Riders' clubrooms. It's been years since we were on friendly terms.

The floor's sticky, and empty beer bottles lay scattered on the floor. A thick layer of dust coats the framed pictures of bikes on the walls. The place stinks of vomit and stale beer, making my nose crinkle.

They don't take pride in their clubhouse the way we do. Maybe this little visit isn't going to hurt them too badly. But it's not about hurting them. It's about letting Manny know we're coming for him, letting him know that I'm out and I want my revenge.

"Anywhere you like. Smash it all to hell."

I swing my bat at the wall, feeling a surge of satisfaction as a portrait of Manny crashes to the ground.

The glass frame shatters, and I don't bother trying to muffle the sound.

The boys let out a whoop and let loose with their bats, swinging wildly at anything and everything.

I reckon we've got about five minutes before someone shows up, and I'm not going to waste that time.

Pulling my shoulder back, I swing as hard as I can, connecting with a pinball machine. It gives a strangled beep as the glass smashes. I hit it again and again, thinking about the last three years.

Three years in prison, locked up and away from my club and away from my daughter, Lily.

It's lucky I had the foresight to add Gina as one of her guardians. I did that ten years ago in case something ever happened to me so they couldn't take my daughter away.

My bat comes down on the legs of the pinball machine, and it gives a whine as a leg gives out and it sinks to its knees.

Smashing shit up feels good. I spin around, looking for my next target.

The room is in chaos with my guys joyfully destroying the clubhouse.

Lyle has rescued a bottle of bourbon from the bar, and he takes a swig before smashing the fridges in.

Someone's gone through to the kitchen, and there's the sound of pots and pans being thrown to the floor.

There's a staircase, and I head up there. I'm looking for the President's room. I want to destroy something that belongs to the man who put me behind bars, that made me miss out on so much of Lily's life.

"That's for missing her prom."

I swing the bat heavily, getting grim satisfaction as it carves a hole in the plaster of the wall.

"And that's for missing her high school graduation."

The bat makes another hole, and this feels fucking good.

Manny put me behind bars. He snitched on me. I was supposed to meet him and his crew for an arms deal. Instead, the cops turned up and caught me with a trunk full of illegal firearms.

I only got a lesser sentence because my sister is the best lawyer in the state.

There's a corridor upstairs with doors leading off to rooms. I try each one, looking for something that Manny would value.

There's a small cupboard at the end, and it's the only door that's locked, which means there must be something worth protecting in there.

I swing my bat hard. It wedges in the door, sending a jolt up my shoulder.

"Motherfucker."

I pull the bat out and swing again. This time, it goes all the way through, making a hole in the door. I reach my hand through, searching for the lock on the other side. My hand finds the doorknob and I turn it, hearing the lock pop open.

There's a rushing sound from the other side of the door, and something comes down on my hand, sending pain shooting up my arm.

"Fuck!" I pull my hand out, and there's blood on my knuckles. Pain sears up my arm, and I see red. Whoever's behind that door is going to pay for this.

My fingers are bent in pain, and I can't grip the baseball bat properly, but I raise it as best I can and open the door.

Someone rushes me. A small ball of fury, hissing at me, all hair and nails, scratching at my arms as they knock me off balance.

I step back, pinned against the other side of the corridor. My bat drops to the floor as I wrestle with the wild cat that's tearing at my skin with her nails.

I know it's a woman because she smells good. Her long hair is wild, and every time it whips around my face, I get a whiff of the floral scent of whatever shampoo she uses.

She's got her legs wrapped around me while her fingers claw at my neck. My head tilts back so she can't scratch my face, and I use my arms to try to wrestle her off. But with my injured hand, it's hard to get a grip on her.

She's fighting with everything she's got, like a cornered animal.

"I'm not gonna hurt you."

I try to calm her down, but it only makes her

more irate. I don't want to hurt her, but I need to get her off me before she finds an eyeball with one of those nails.

"I need you to calm down."

I try to warn her, but she still gives a surprised oomph when I drop to my knees and roll her onto the floor.

Now I'm pinning her down, holding her still with my one good arm. Her hair falls off her face, and for the first time, I get a proper look at my attacker.

She's got full, youthful lips, deep red where she's been biting them. Her skin is smooth and tanned, and her wide, dark eyes cast around the room wildly.

My breath catches in my throat. My blood roars in my ears.

Mine.

The word echoes in my head, pounds in my heart, and reverberates through my very soul.

Mine, Mine, Mine.

It's a clear chant in my head that I'm sure she must hear. And maybe she does because her eyes find mine. She stills for a moment, and we stare at each other.

Her look is pure terror, and a flash of anger

goes through me, wondering what she's so frightened off.

"I'm not going to hurt you."

I keep my voice steady and calm, like how you'd talk to a frightened animal, and it seems to work.

Her eyes stay on me, and her breathing slows. I can feel the swell of her breasts under me with each ragged breath. And help me, God, but I can't help but glance down to peek at the soft mounds that are billowing up and down as she breathes.

Her top has come unbuttoned, and the white lace of her bra is on show, framing two soft pillowy breasts.

My body responds instantly. And she must feel it because the fight comes back into her. She kicks her knee up, and I duck out the way before she can get me in the goods.

The woman rolls out from under me, and I grab her by the ankle before she can escape. She gives a whimper as I drag her back and pin her under me again.

This time, I pin her legs down with my thighs as I hold her hands over her head.

She looks beautiful splayed out on the ground. More than beautiful. The blood rushes south, and I have to look away. I have to block the sight of her below me, the scent of her filling my nostrils. Because I'm not an animal and because I recognize this girl. Although she's not a girl anymore, now clearly a woman. She's Scarlett, Manny's daughter.

"I'm not going to hurt you, Scarlett."

Her eyes widen when I say her name, and her nostrils flare. "My father will find you."

She spits the words with such venom that spittle lands on my lips. I flick my tongue out, tasting her on me. Salty and sweet.

"I'm counting on it."

She breathes hard, but when I help her to her feet, she doesn't resist.

Keeping one hand grasped around Scarlett's wrists, I look into what I thought was a closet, the room where Scarlett was hiding. There's a mattress on the floor and a shelf with a few books and a small stack of folded clothes.

"This your room?"

She sticks her chin out defiantly, not giving me an answer. But the way her cheeks flush red tells me everything I need to know.

Manny lets his daughter sleep in a closet. The guy doesn't deserve her.

The sounds of crashing from downstairs have

faded, and Jesse appears at the top of the stairs. "Time to go, Pres."

"I guess I'll be the one who has to clean this mess up," Scarlett huffs.

"Not this time, darling."

I lift her off her feet, and she gives a squeal. She's curvy but she's short, and I toss her over my shoulder like a sack of potatoes.

"What are you doing?" Scarlett gives an indignant huff.

I don't answer her because it's obvious what I'm doing. I'm taking her.

"Put me down." Scarlett wriggles on my shoulder, and her small fists pummel my back. I stride down the stairs to where the guys are waiting.

"Who's the girl?" Lyle asks.

I wrap my arms around Scarlett's jean-clad thighs, pinning her in place.

"She's my revenge."

To keep reading visit:
mybook.to/UCBikersRevenge

GET YOUR FREE BOOK

Sign up to the Sadie King mailing list for a FREE book!

You'll be the first to hear about exclusive offers, bonus content and all the news from Sadie King.

To claim your free book visit:
www.authorsadieking.com/free

Sadie King is a USA Today Best Selling Author of short instalove romance.

She lives in New Zealand with her ex-military husband and raucous young son.

When she's not writing she loves catching waves with her son, running along the beach, and good wine, preferably drunk with a book in hand.

Keep in touch when you sign up for her newsletter. You'll even snag yourself a free short romance!

www.authorsadieking.com/free

* 9 7 9 8 2 1 5 1 4 8 4 7 1 *